The use of too many questions has been avoided, as it is more important to encourage comment and discussion than to expect particular answers.

Care has been taken to retain sufficient realism in the illustrations and subject matter to enable a young child to have fun identifying objects, creatures and situations.

It is wise to remember that patience and understanding are very important, and that children do not all develop evenly or at the same rate. Parents should not be anxious if children do not give correct answers to those questions that are asked. With help, they will do so in their own time.

The brief notes at the back of this book will enable interested parents to make the fullest use of these **Ladybird talkabout** books.

Ladybird Books

**compiled by** Margaret West and Ethel Wingfield

**illustrated by** Harry Wingfield

The publishers wish to acknowledge the assistance of the nursery school advisers who helped with the preparation of this book.

Published by Ladybird Books Ltd  Loughborough  Leicestershire  UK
Ladybird Books Inc  Lewiston  Maine 04240  USA

# talkabout
# starting
# school

# You will have lots of new friends

You may have
your own drawer
and your own bag
for your own things

There is a peg
for your coat . .

## . . you can go to the lavatory

## . . and you can wash your hands

# **Find** the peg
with this picture on

Here are som

. . and this

. . and this

# School pets must be looked after

It may be a rabbit
or a gerbil

or some fish,
or a guinea-pig

or just the
school cat

Here are some things
you use at school

# You will paint and make things

# Everybody goes out to play

# You will learn about **sounds**

dog

cow

hen

cat

# Can you find this sound again?

a

b

and this?

f

e

and this?

d

g

# p a

# f t

# o d

What other sounds do you know?

# You will **sort** and **weigh**

# You will **count** and **measure**

Number jigsaws

**Find** another number like this

4

2

and this

3

5

and this

6

9

How old are you

1 4

8 3

6 7

Can you point to the number?

Most children
have dinner
at school

# Some people who help you at school

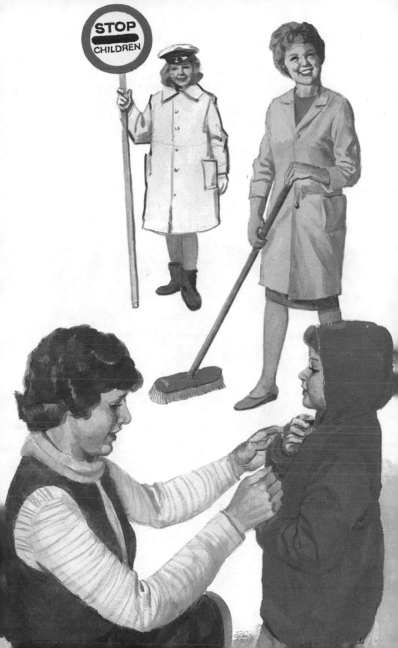

# You can play house and dress up

You will sing and
make music

# Sometimes you will cook

# Everybody dances

ou may go out, perhaps to the Zo

ometimes you will
listen to a story

Tell the story

# Suggestions for extending the use of this **talkabout** book . . .

The page headings are only brief suggestions as to how the illustrations may be used. However, these illustrations have been planned to help children to understand various important concepts during their discussions with you.

Starting school is the child's first step towards independence. If he can be helped by a little preparation and by giving him some idea of what will be required of him, this big step can be taken much more easily. That is the main purpose of this book.

Additionally, most head teachers will invite parent and child to visit the school before